Hello Kitty

and friends

The Winter Wonderland

·A HELLO KITTY ADVENTURE·

Hello Kitty

and friends

The Winter Wonderland
·A HELLO KITTY ADVENTURE·

MEET Hello Kitty and friends

Hello Kitty

Mimmy

Tammy

Mama

Papa

Grandpa

Grandma

Fifi

Dear Daniel

With special thanks to
Linda Chapman and Michelle Misra

First published in Great Britain by HarperCollins Children's Books in 2015

www.harpercollins.co.uk
1 3 5 7 9 10 8 6 4 2

ISBN: 978-0-00-754246-8

Printed and bound in England by Clays Ltd, St Ives plc.

MIX
Paper from
responsible sources
FSC® C007454

FSC™ is a non-profit international organisation established to promote
the responsible management of the world's forests. Products carrying the
FSC label are independently certified to assure consumers that they come
from forests that are managed to meet the social, economic and
ecological needs of present and future generations,
and other controlled sources.

Find out more about HarperCollins and the environment at
www.harpercollins.co.uk/green

Contents

Let It Snow!

Hello Kitty looked out the window of her

sitting room. Perfect white snowflakes were

flurrying down, settling on the garden. She felt

a shiver of excitement fizzle through her. There

was just one week left till Christmas and already

it had started to snow! How SUPER was that!

Not so super, though, was her broken leg, which was propped up on a cushion in front of her. It had been in a cast now for four weeks – ever since she had landed badly in a gymnastics competition and broken it.

Hello Kitty let out a little sigh. Still, at least it meant she had the chance to make Christmas cards for Dear Daniel, Tammy and Fifi.

Hello Kitty *smiled* as she thought about her friends – her very best friends in the whole world. Together they made up the Friendship Club – a club that met after school and in the holidays to do all sorts of fun things like baking and painting and visiting fun places!

Hello Kitty *and friends*

Today the rest of the Friendship Club were out ice-skating. Hello Kitty couldn't go because of her broken leg but her friends had *promised* to call in afterwards. She checked the clock; she really should get on with their cards…

Hello Kitty pulled out a box and tipped it out over the table in front of her. There were:

Glitter pens

Cotton wool

Starry stickers

Glue

GLUE

And everything else she'd need to make the best Christmas cards ever!

Hello Kitty set to work.
Dear Daniel loved animals so
she drew some reindeer for
him and filled it in with **lots**

of glitter.

For Fifi she was going

to make a picture of an

ice-skater using cotton

wool for

the snow,

and for Tammy she

was going to draw a Christmas

fairy with **sparkly** wings!

At that moment
Hello Kitty's twin
sister, Mimmy, came
in and offered to
help. She sat down,
and soon they were
cutting and pasting
and sprinkling glitter and
having a whole lot of fun together. So much fun
that they nearly didn't hear the doorbell ring!

Quickly, they shuffled the Christmas cards
away. They didn't want their friends to see the
cards before they were finished. That would spoil
the surprise!

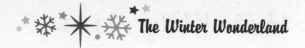

Mimmy ran into the hall and opened the door, and Hello Kitty's friends spilled inside, talking and laughing. They pulled off their coats and hats and gloves and soon all *sorts* of winter things were scattered everywhere. Once they were done they rushed into the sitting room, all of them talking at once.

The ice rink had been outside – right in front of the Winter Wonderland, Dear Daniel told her – the park that had been set up to run through the winter months. They hadn't gone inside, Tammy burst out, but they had seen *all* of the rides and gift stalls and things to eat. Not only that, but the Winter Wonderland had real reindeer and a Santa's grotto as well!

Hello Kitty thought it sounded brilliant! She hoped they'd be able to visit some time over Christmas – if she ever got this cast off her leg… soon!

Tammy smiled and asked Hello Kitty what she had been doing. Hello Kitty told her that she had been having fun making Christmas cards with Mimmy.

Phew! Her friends looked relieved. They had been worried she might have been feeling miserable stuck inside the house. They wanted to go carol singing the next day but with Hello Kitty stuck inside… Hello Kitty smiled and told them to stop worrying! She had the Christmas tree to decorate, and she didn't want her friends missing out on fun just because she couldn't join in.

She grinned at them. Besides, didn't they have some work to do for her?

The rest of the Friendship Club looked puzzled as she pointed out of the window. Hello Kitty explained that it was the **perfect** weather for making a snowman, and she wanted one in her own garden!

Of course! Everyone giggled as her friends put on their winter clothes and went outside again. Soon they were having snowball fights and making the biggest snowman they could. Hello Kitty watched them from inside, **smiling** and waving.

Hello Kitty *and friends*

After a while though, everyone started to look cold! Hello Kitty thought they might be in need of a hot drink to warm them up.

She called Mama, who agreed and went into the kitchen. The Friendship Club came in, and soon they were all drinking delicious hot chocolate with whipped cream. *Yummy!*

They were so freezing cold it took them quite a while to warm up their fingers and toes. At least that was one thing Hello Kitty hadn't minded missing out on!

The next day was bright and cold, and

Hello Kitty was just about to start making some

Christmas punch when the doorbell rang. Her

friends were back early from carol singing!

Dear Daniel, Fifi and Tammy rushed in.

Hello Kitty wanted to show

them what she had been up

to. Proudly, she pointed out

the racks of pies and cookies

she had made that morning with Mama. And
not only had she been baking, she said, but she
had also helped Mama and Mimmy decorate the
Christmas tree.

Ta da! She pointed at a beautifully
decorated tree right beside the fireplace. It had
little balls and tinsel decorating it from top to toe.
Pretty fairy lights twinkled all over and at the very
top sat a Christmas angel. Dear Daniel, Tammy
and Fifi thought it looked absolutely SUPER!

So how had their morning been? Hello Kitty
asked.

Well... Fifi could hardly contain herself.
While they had been carol singing they had seen

a poster, and there was going to be a Christmas parade – the very next night! Everyone was going to dress up as Christmas characters and there would be singing and dancing as they walked through the streets. Not only that, but there was going to be a prize for the best costume, too! They had to get to **work** immediately. There wasn't much time! But what should they go as? It would have to

be something that they could all do, so that

everyone could take part. Hello Kitty felt a bit

sad. Not **everyone,** she pointed out. She

had a pair of crutches for around the house, but

there was no way she could manage a long walk

around the town. She wouldn't be able to take

part in the parade.

Oh dear.

Her friends said quickly

that they wouldn't

take part in the parade

without her, but Hello

Kitty told them they

mustn't be silly.

Of course they HAD to take part. She would join in by helping them make the best costumes ever!

Dear Daniel, Tammy and Fifi grinned at each other in relief. Hello Kitty smiled – they should get started right then and there! But what should they dress as? Hmmmm…

Ah ha – Hello Kitty had an idea! What about angels? They could drape white sheets over themselves, decorated with stars, and she was sure that her mother wouldn't mind them borrowing some left over

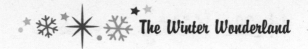

tinsel to use as belts and to make halos with!

Quickly, the four friends started cutting and

pasting... And *eating* all the cookies and

mince pies too!

They were just about to start on the halos when the doorbell rang. It was time for everyone to go home. There wouldn't be time to finish everything now; they would just have to do it tomorrow. Still, they were *almost* done! The angel costumes glittered and sparkled in the lights of the tree.

Hello Kitty got up to show their parents what they had done while Fifi, Tammy and Dear Daniel  were left looking from one to the other. They were pleased that

Hello Kitty was helping with their costumes, but **surely** there had to be a way that she could take part in the parade as well? It would be so much more fun if she was with them. But just what *could* they do?

Secrets

Hello Kitty held the phone in her hand the next day, waiting for Fifi to answer it. She was hoping that her friend would come over to help finish off the costumes for the parade and make the halos as well.

At last! Fifi was as friendly as always, but Hello Kitty felt like there was something wrong. And no, Fifi couldn't come over that afternoon.

Hello Kitty wanted to ask why Fifi was so **busy** and what she was doing, but Fifi had hung up the phone. Hmmmm – she'd try to call Tammy next instead. But when she phoned Tammy's house,

Tammy's mother said

that she was already out.

Which left Dear Daniel.

There was no answer there

either.

Oh well! Hello Kitty would just have to get on

with the costumes on her own.

She had just started on the halos when she

realised she would need Fifi to measure her head so

she could get her size. She'd give her another call.

Brring… Brrrring… Hello Kitty bit her lip as

she waited for Fifi to answer. There she was now.

Quickly, Hello Kitty explained what she

needed – to measure Fifi's head so she would

know how big to make her halo! Easy.

Oh… Fifi went quiet.

What was it?

Fifi explained that there was no *need* for

Hello Kitty to bother about the halos anymore.

They'd decided to change their costumes and

wouldn't need halos for them.

Oh… Hello Kitty felt tears prickle in her eyes. After all the time they'd put into making the costumes – she had thought that everyone had liked the idea as much as

her. She was *about* to ask Fifi what the new ones were when she heard something in the background… It sounded like voices.

Quickly, Fifi told her that had to go! She said she would explain later and before Hello Kitty

could say anything more, she was left holding the
quiet phone in her hand. Fifi was gone.

Hello Kitty slowly put the phone down.
What was going on? Why was Fifi being so
strange? And she was sure it had been Tammy
and Dear Daniel's voices that she had heard in
the background. Hello Kitty took a **deep**
breath. She felt very left out.

At that moment Mimmy appeared behind her.
Hello Kitty told Mimmy what
had happened – that she was
sure that her friends had
all been together, without
her, and keeping it a secret.

She didn't really feel like going to watch them

in the parade now! But Mimmy thought that

Hello Kitty must be imagining things. Her friends

would **never** be like that.

Hello Kitty supposed that Mimmy was right.

She would go. She wouldn't let her friends down!

Surprise, Surprise!

That evening, Hello Kitty got dressed up in

warm clothing and stood by the door on her

crutches as she waited for Mimmy and their

parents.

Eventually they came down the stairs, all

bundled up too. Hello Kitty could see Mimmy's costume *peeking* out of her coat – a pink tutu and white fake fur wrap. She was going as the Sugar Plum fairy! Hello Kitty smiled; it suited Mimmy perfectly. Mama and Papa White told the girls that they were going to drive over to the start of the parade, so that Hello Kitty could sit at the organisers' table and watch from there. **Perfect!**

As Hello Kitty hopped outside on her crutches and took a big deep breath of the crisp

winter air, she looked up to see Tammy, Fifi and

Dear Daniel coming through the front gate.

What was going on? They were pulling a green

sledge, decorated all over with lots of ribbons,

tinsel and presents.

Surprise! They all grinned and called out. They had decorated the sledge especially for Hello Kitty, they told her, so that she could take part in the parade as well – they were going to pull her! That was **why** they had had to change their costumes – so that they could be reindeer instead!

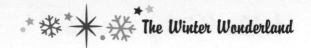

Hello Kitty looked at what her friends were wearing and saw that instead of angels, they were dressed as snow-white reindeer, with antlers instead of halos, and Dear Daniel was all in brown with a red nose. He was the most important reindeer of all – Rudolph!

Hello Kitty's eyes
widened. They had
done all this for her? It
was absolutely SUPER!
She grinned at her
friends and told them all how **wonderful**

they looked. Fifi and Tammy were perfect dressed

up as reindeer, and Dear Daniel looked fantastic

as Rudolph. She was going to look very out of

place in her normal clothes. Oh well!

But oh no she wasn't – **TA DA!** Her

friends held out a little red costume. Hello Kitty

couldn't believe it. They had made a little red

Santa suit for her with the softest white fake

fur collar, a brown belt, and big black boots

that would fit over her cast. Wow! Hello Kitty

couldn't wait to put everything on.

Her friends hugged her. All of the whispering

and the phone calls hadn't been them leaving her

out at all. They had just been doing something

nice for her to make sure she could take part

in the parade too! They'd wanted to keep it a

surprise. Hello Kitty **grinned** at everyone;

this was going to be the best parade ever. And

all because her friends were the best – the very

best in the whole world!

There wasn't a moment to lose. The parade was starting soon – Hello Kitty wedged herself on to the sledge and Dear Daniel, Fifi and Tammy stood in the ropes in front of her. Was she ready? You *bet* she was. They picked up the ropes and started to pull, stamping and tossing their heads like real reindeer.

Around them, the streets were full of people who had turned up to watch the parade, as well as others in costume ready to walk in it – there were snowmen and Santas and angels and elves. There were people dressed up as Christmas trees and Christmas puddings, and even presents as well!

It was **cold**, but as pretty as a picture and the excitement was keeping Hello Kitty warm. She looked over to the side

where Mimmy stood as the Sugar Plum fairy;
Hello Kitty couldn't have felt more Christmassy
if she had tried!

Hello Kitty and her friends started singing as
they pulled the sledge down the streets. As they
passed the crowds that had come out to watch
everyone cheered, and Hello Kitty thought to
herself that it was the most magical night ever.

It was clear and bright and little stars twinkled in the sky.

As the parade came into the town square, a **big** Christmas tree stretched high into the sky, lights twinkling on it from top to bottom. A stage had been set up next to it and all the

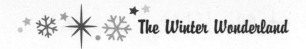
crowds were gathering around as a man on the

stage started to speak. He began by saying what

a success the evening had been, and how it had

raised a **huge** amount of money for charity!

They hadn't finished counting everything up yet,

but when they had it was going to be used to

make sure that everyone would have a proper

Christmas dinner and a present too. The crowd

gave a loud cheer.

But before he sent everyone on their way,

he had to announce the prize for the **best**

costume. This year it was going to a group of

friends who had gone to lots of trouble so that

their other friend could take part, and that was

really what Christmas was all about. And that

group was… The Friendship Club!

He pointed over to the sledge where Dear

Daniel, Tammy and Fifi were standing, with

Hello Kitty behind, and everyone gave a **loud**

cheer! Hello Kitty beamed as her friends climbed

up on to the stage to collect the prize of a bright

red envelope.

They waited till they were back with

Hello Kitty and gave it to her to open.

She tore it open *quickly* – tickets to

Winter Wonderland! To

be used whenever they

wanted. Hooray! They were

WINTER WONDERLAND
ENTRANCE
TICKET
ADMIT ONE

all going to be able to go to visit the park –

Mimmy too because there was one extra ticket.

Hello Kitty beamed at her friends. Could they

go next week when the cast would be off her leg?

Her friends grinned. Of course they could!

Hooray to that too! As the Friendship Club

stood in the lights of the Christmas tree, they all

agreed – it was going to be the best Christmas

EVER!

A Day Out

Hello Kitty bounced excitedly in her seat in the back of the car. It was Christmas Eve and her leg had been out of her plaster cast for just a couple of days! It was still a bit wobbly but getting better every day. Now she and

Mimmy were on the way to meet the rest of

the Friendship Club at the Winter Wonderland.

They were talking about the most exciting thing

they would be doing on their visit…GOING TO

SANTA'S GROTTO TO SEE SANTA!

Mama White listened in and glanced over her

shoulder. There would even be reindeer, and

people dressed up as elves to show them the

way there, she said… Hello Kitty and Mimmy

looked at each other – elves! How *super!*

Hello Kitty thought to herself

that she'd love to dress up as an

elf and help people when she

was older.

They arrived at the Winter Wonderland car park at last, and the girls jumped out after Mama parked the car. It hadn't **stopped** snowing all week and everywhere looked very pretty. Looking at the blanket of white on the ground, Hello Kitty was reminded of the icing sugar on one of Grandma White's Christmas cakes.

It even looked like it might snow again that afternoon, but Hello Kitty and Mimmy didn't mind. They **loved** snow! They hurried towards the entrance with Mama behind – it was great to run now that Hello Kitty didn't have to use her crutches any more. There was an enormous Christmas tree beside the entrance, covered in sparkling lights… SURPRISE!

Dear Daniel, Fifi and Tammy all jumped out from behind the Christmas tree. Hello Kitty and Mimmy both squealed, and Hello Kitty slipped on the snow and fell over! **Oh no!**

Hello Kitty *and friends*

Everyone ran to help her up — they didn't want

her to break her leg again! Hello Kitty giggled at

her friends' worried faces. She was fine. Mama

sorted out the tickets and smiled at them all —

were they ready to go inside?

There was only one answer to that —

OF COURSE!

The Friendship Club hurried in through the gate and found themselves in an enormous hall, with walls covered with tinsel and sparkling lights, and lots of stalls selling Christmas gifts. There were roasting chestnuts and people handing out hot drinks, and the air smelled of gingerbread and fresh pine – *yum!*

Hello Kitty gazed round. There were people everywhere; children **laughing**, parents with buggies, grandparents smiling happily. She grinned at her friends; this really was the perfect way to spend Christmas Eve!

Fifi grinned back. What did everyone want to do first?

60

Hello Kitty knew exactly what SHE wanted to do. She really wanted to go into the gardens and see the reindeer, and find Santa's grotto. But luckily, that's what everyone else wanted to do too! Waving goodbye to Mama, they *ran* through the hall and out into the snowy garden…

5

Snowstorm!

In the Winter Wonderland gardens, the snow was white and beautiful and the frosty air stung Hello Kitty's cheeks. There was a small ice skating rink filled with people, and a sign with an arrow on it: SANTA'S GROTTO THIS WAY.

The arrow pointed into the woods, where a path of wooden boards had been put down through the trees so that it was easier for people with buggies or wheelchairs. Twinkling fairy lights had been strung from the branches of the trees on either side of the path. It looked very magical.

They headed towards the path, but just then Tammy spotted a paddock where eight brown and white reindeer were munching on a big pile of hay. They had big antlers and thick shaggy coats, and there was a **big** red sleigh next to the paddock piled high with presents and decorated with tinsel!

Hello Kitty *and friends*

The Friendship Club ran over to where a man was brushing one of the reindeer. He **smiled** and gave them some treats that the reindeer liked, and as the reindeer came over Hello Kitty took off her gloves so she could feel their soft coats.

They nuzzled her
hands to eat the
treats and looked
at her with gentle
brown eyes; she

thought they were the most beautiful animals she

had ever seen!

Dear Daniel asked if the reindeer pulled the

sleigh that was by the gate, and the man told

them that the reindeer *could* pull it, but it was

just being used for decoration at the moment.

The presents on it weren't real, but if they went

to Santa's grotto then they would all get a real

present there!

Mimmy pulled Hello Kitty's arm and pointed.
Four people dressed as elves were walking
out of the woods. They were wearing **cute**
costumes – a green skirt and top with a big belt,
tights, black boots and green hats! Hello Kitty
wished she had a costume like that too!

Just then a snowflake floated down out of
the sky and landed on Fifi's nose – she sneezed
and they all **giggled**. But it
was followed by another
and then another…
Snowflakes were
suddenly swirling out of
the clouds. Oh dear!

There was going to be a snowstorm! They had better take cover inside for the moment. Hopefully the snow would stop soon and then the elves could take them to see Santa in his grotto.

Everyone **squeezed** back into the hall; it was so warm inside that they had to take off their coats and hats and gloves! They found Mama and left them with her, and went to explore the stalls.

Hello Kitty had a small red purse full of money. She listened to her friends chatting as they

walked around, and then snuck off to buy their

Christmas presents. She bought…

A book about a

A snow globe for Fifi   penguin for Tammy

A picture of a reindeer for

Dear Daniel

There! All her Christmas shopping was done!

She already had presents for her family. When everyone else had finished their shopping they stopped for a hot chocolate. Fifi looked out of the window to **see** if the snow had stopped yet... But no. It was STILL swirling down.

What could they do? Just then there was a loud

voice over the speakers asking for quiet as the

carol signers were about to start! *Perfect*...

the Friendship Club all settled down to listen. The

sweet singing put big smiles on everyone's faces,

until, glancing out the window, Tammy gave a cry.

Hello Kitty and friends

At last! The snow had stopped. They started to go outside to finally see Santa, but Hello Kitty saw the elf helpers just by the back door, looking very worried. *What* was wrong?

Hello Kitty went over to check, and a very pretty elf girl told her the snow had completely covered the path that led to

Santa's grotto, and now no one would be able
to get there at all – **Oh no!** Whatever could
they do? This really was a disaster.

Hello Kitty *and friends*

Winter Wonderland wouldn't be nearly so much **fun** without a visit to Santa! Hello Kitty knew that all the visitors would be very disappointed.

Hello Kitty went back to tell the Friendship Club. They all wished there was something they

could do to help, and thought

hard. Then Dear Daniel noticed

a spade leaning against the

wall… **Maybe** they could

all dig the snow from the path

to clear it? If they worked together it might

not take too long – and the Friendship Club

were very good at

working together!

Hello Kitty quickly

ran to tell the elves,

and as she told

them the idea, their

faces lit up.

It could *definitely* help if they all worked together! All the elves hurried to find some more spades.

Everyone put on their outdoor clothes again and told Mama where they were going as the

elves hurried back with the spades. They all stomped outside to start – the children had to be able to get to see Santa!

They began to clear the snow from the path that led across the garden and into the woods. It was **hard** work though!

Soon they had cleared the path that led across
the garden. They started clearing the path that
led through the woods – but *oh no!*

As they went round the first corner they saw that a rotten tree had fallen across the path, its branches weighed down from so much snow. Dear Daniel climbed over it — but *what* about the children in buggies or the people in wheelchairs? They wouldn't be able to get past it at all. But what could they all do?

Everyone put down their spades and scratched their heads.

They tried to move the tree themselves, but it was just **too** heavy. What else could they try, Mimmy wondered aloud – was there another way through the forest? An elf explained that there was, but without the wooden pathway the snow would be too **deep** to push buggies or wheelchairs through. The wheels would sink into the snow.

There really seemed to be no way through. They headed inside sadly, to tell everyone the bad news…

But as they came out of the woods,

Hello Kitty saw the reindeer and **gasped**.

She'd had an idea! Couldn't the reindeer pull the

big sleigh? It would slip easily across deep snow.

People could ride on it and visit Santa that way!

What did everyone *think?*

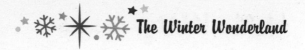

They all started talking excitedly. It was a SUPER idea!

The elves said they would go inside and make an announcement, and the man looking after the reindeer said they would enjoy it – the reindeer L♥VED pulling the sleigh! He would need to get the sleigh cleared and the reindeer harnessed up though. Tammy and Fifi grinned and asked if he would like some help. He smiled and nodded. The more the merrier!

The Friendship Club sprang into action.

First they cleared the presents off the sleigh

and Tammy and Mimmy cleaned it while Dear

Daniel, Fifi and Hello Kitty helped harness up

the reindeer. There were **lots** of buckles to

do up. The reindeer tossed their antlers excitedly and stamped their hooves. They seemed to know what was happening!

They fastened the reindeer to the sleigh; the reins *even* had bells on them so that the sleigh tinkled as it moved, and then they were ready –

the man got into the driving seat and the Friendship Club jumped on board! It was time to pick up some passengers. He shook the reins and they set off towards the hall. The sleigh slid smoothly across the snow, the bells jingling. Hello Kitty grinned at Mimmy – this was *definitely* the best way to travel on a snowy day!

A queue of people were waiting by the door with the elves. The little children were looking

very excited – they hadn't expected they would

have a special sleigh ride that afternoon.

Hello Kitty and the others *jumped* off to let

everyone else go to Santa's grotto first. The elves

helped the children on to the sleigh and the

grown-ups got ready to walk beside

it. Mama had fetched some

warm and cosy blankets

from inside and the

Friendship Club tucked

everyone in, before the

man shook the reins,

the bells tinkled, and

off the sleigh went!

Hello Kitty and friends

Hello Kitty and the Friendship Club **waved** the first load of passengers away.

After a little while the sleigh came back with some very happy children all clutching brightly coloured presents, and then it was time for the second load of people to go and visit Santa. The sleigh made trip after trip. By the time the last group of people got back from the grotto, the sun was setting in the sky. But at least everyone had been to see Santa – everyone apart from the Friendship Club that is!

A smiley girl dressed as an elf turned to the

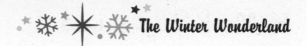

Friendship Club – it was their turn now! They

had helped save the day and she knew Santa was

really looking forward to meeting them. Hello

Kitty and the others exchanged excited looks.

What was Santa going to be like? They couldn't **wait** to find out!

They climbed on to the sleigh and tucked the blankets over their knees. There was even room for Mama to ride with them too.

The reindeer moved off,
and the Friendship Club
clutched each other's hands.
They were **off** to Santa's
grotto, finally – HOORAY!

6

Santa's Grotto

The sleigh slid across the thick snow and into

the trees. It was dusk inside the woods now and

the fairy lights **twinkled**, lighting their path. The

bells on the sleigh jingled. Every time Hello Kitty

breathed out, her breath froze in a white cloud

on the air. As they went deeper into the woods,

Hello Kitty felt her heart beating faster.

What would Santa be

like?

Mimmy squeezed her

hand; she was excited too!

Look! Fifi pointed through the trees. Just

ahead of them was a little wooden cabin. Golden

light was spilling out of the windows and long

icicles hung down from the roof. There was a

holly wreath on the little door and two elves

waiting beside it. The sleigh stopped, and the elf

helpers helped Mama and the Friendship Club

down. They whispered that they had told Santa

SANTA'S GROTTO

all about how the Friendship Club had helped –

and he wanted to say *thank you!*

They knocked on the door and a deep voice

told them to come in; Hello Kitty led the way

inside and everyone crowded in behind her.

The hut was warm and
cosy with a circular rug,
a fireplace, a Christmas
tree and sacks of
presents.
Santa was sitting in
a chair beside the
fireplace. He had
a very long white
beard and was really

tall, with big black boots and a big round belly!
He gave them a twinkly smile. So *this* was the
Friendship Club who had helped everyone today!
He had heard all about them.

For once no one in
the Friendship Club
seemed to know
what to say. It was
AMAZING to
be standing there
with Santa, deep in
the middle of the woods
with the reindeer outside, stamping in the snow.
They gazed at him in wonder and he gave them
all a big smile. He had some special presents for
them, he said, to say a big thank you for saving
the day at Winter Wonderland – he hoped the
presents would always help them to remember

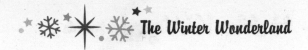

how they had been his special helpers. He

reached into a sack at his feet and handed each

of them a present wrapped in red and green

tissue paper with a **big** bow on it. They all said

thank you and Mama and Santa smiled. Santa told

them not to forget to leave out their stockings

and pillowcases that night. He had a feeling they

might find some more presents in the morning!

But now it was time to go – Santa had work to do! The Friendship Club all waved goodbye and then went back outside and got into the sleigh. As the reindeer pulled them back to the hall they **all** started to talk at once. Hadn't Santa been wonderful? He had been just like they had always imagined him! It had been lovely to be able to help him.

Mama said she was very proud of them all, and Hello Kitty asked if they could open their presents. Mama smiled and nodded. She was *sure* Santa wouldn't mind if they opened one present a day early... They all ripped the tissue paper off quickly, and Hello Kitty squealed so loudly that two of the reindeer **jumped!** Santa had given them all perfect little elf costumes! Wow – SUPER!

Hello Kitty held up the little green costume and hat. She couldn't wait to get home and try it on. Everyone else was **delighted** with their costumes too. They would never forget helping Santa now! The sleigh stopped outside the hall, which was still lit up brightly even though the rest of Winter Wonderland was starting to

empty — everyone was going home to get ready for Christmas Day. Hello Kitty and her friends **hugged** and patted all the reindeer; it was time

for them to go to their big warm

barn for the night where they

had a thick bed of straw and a

manger of hay.

Mama smiled. It was time

for Hello Kitty and her friends

to go home too – after

all, there were stockings

to put up. And milk and

cookies for Santa and carrots

for the reindeer to put out too, put in

Fifi! Everyone giggled and agreed;

they couldn't forget that after

today!

The Friendship Club said goodbye to the elf helpers and skipped to the car park together, clutching their presents and parcels. Hello Kitty thought it had been the best Christmas Eve ever, and it had even made her think up another new Friendship Club rule:

Good friends always work together to make sure no one is left out – not even Santa!

The others laughed and agreed and hugged each other goodbye. They would see each other the next day because everyone was coming round to Hello Kitty and Mimmy's house to swap presents in the afternoon.

Hello Kitty and Mimmy got into the car and

waved goodbye as Mama started the car to drive them home. Stars were just starting to twinkle in the dark sky and just for a moment, Hello Kitty was SURE she saw a sleigh soaring up above the trees… She smiled happily to herself and sighed. Merry Christmas – and a Super New Year to everyone!

The end

**Turn over the page for activities and fun
things that you can do with your friends
– just like Hello Kitty!**

Make Candy Cane photo ornaments!

Christmas time is all about family and friends, so what better way to celebrate than with these Candy Cane photo frame ornaments – hang them on your tree so you can see all your loved ones every Christmas day! You will need a grown-up's help to make these.

You will need:

Glue

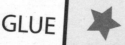

GLUE

Coloured felt – red and green are nice and Christmassy!

**Candy canes
(2 for each frame)**

Scissors

**Photographs of family and
friends – check to make sure
these are ones you can cut up!**

**Coloured ribbon to hang your
frames (approximately 20cm for
each frame)**

Glitter to decorate

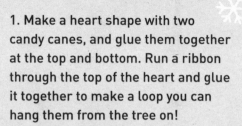

1. Make a heart shape with two candy canes, and glue them together at the top and bottom. Run a ribbon through the top of the heart and glue it together to make a loop you can hang them from the tree on!

2. When the glue is dry, trace around the heart shape on two pieces of felt, and cut them out.

3. Cut a window in one piece of felt, big enough to see your photo through! Cut the photo to size so it will fit.

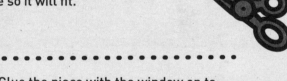

4. Glue the piece with the window on to the candy canes, put your photo in place, and glue the second heart shape on to the back.

5. Decorate with glitter, and you have a beautiful framed picture to hang on your tree – Hooray!

COLLECT
ALL OF THE

Hello Kitty

and friends
STORIES

The Friendship Club · The School Trip · The Summer Fair · The Pop Princess · The Wedding Day · The Beach Holiday · The Treasure Hunt

The Talent Show · The Christmas Present · The TV Star · The Big Race · The Makeover Party · The Animal Adventure · The Halloween Parade

The Magazine Mix-Up · The Cupcake Mystery · The Dance Camp · The Camping Trip · The Big Bake Off · The Winter Wonderland

      ✔

Collect them all!

Hello Kitty's Secret Word

Can you find the words below in the grid? When you have found them, the remaining letters will reveal a secret word!

TREE	SANTA
SNOW	ARROW
ANGEL	

S	A	N	T	A
N	R	T	R	N
O	R	I	E	G
W	O	N	E	E
S	W	E	L	L

The Secret Word is:

S N O W S L